Entertaining Angels

a novella

Lawrence Balleine

Parson's Porch Books

www.parsonsporchbooks.com

Entertaining Angels

ISBN: Softcover 978-1-949888-85-0

Copyright © 2019 by Lawrence Balleine

All rights reserved. No part of this book may be reproduced or transmitted in any form or by any means, electronic or mechanical, including photocopying, recording, or by any information storage and retrieval system, without permission in writing from the publisher.

Entertaining Angels

MICHAEL FELT COMPELLED to turn off Highway N and proceed up the long gravel driveway. He was on the third day of his two-week, late June escapade when he spotted it. It was a farmhouse that looked just like his childhood home. He had to have a closer look. Not being in a hurry, making the stop was no problem.

Michael had finalized plans for his trip a couple of months earlier. His goal was to meander through the state of Wisconsin and visit with several farmers along the way. He wanted to find out firsthand how the changes that had been occurring in agriculture during the past twenty-five to thirty years were affecting rural folks, especially dairy farmers.

Michael Lattimore had grown up in rural Wisconsin amid a sea of dairy farms. He had left the state following his graduation from college. He finally returned to live in the Badger state after an absence of thirty years when he landed a teaching position at Gardner Middle School in Green Bay. It was then that it stuck him. So many changes on the rural landscape. Barns that had been occupied by cattle and stocked with hay bales now stood empty. Much of the pastureland was now producing soybeans or corn. The rectangular bales of his youth weighing 50 to 60 pounds and bound by twine had been replaced with huge round bales that had to be moved with a front-end loader. The tractors and equipment had become massive. Whereas over 90,000 dairy farms were operating in Wisconsin during his high school days, only about 10,000 remained. Several of the family dairy farms that milked fifty or so cows ceased to exist, while mega-farms whose herds numbered in the hundreds and sometimes thousands were now appearing. And cows that had been pastured now spent their time roaming about in free-stall sheds.

Stunned by so much that was different, Michael wanted to learn how these changes were affecting the lives of those close to the land; in particular, the family farmer.

Having been a social studies teacher for over a quarter of a century, Michael had met his wife, Elaine, while doing graduate studies at Kent State in Ohio. Upon the completion of their degrees, they were fortunate to find teaching positions in Dublin, a suburb of Columbus. Michael was hired to teach American history at the local high school, and Elaine began her career as a fourth-grade teacher. But after about twenty years, Michael's parent's health was failing, and he wanted to get closer to them. He began to look for a position back home in Wisconsin. Fortunately, he was hired as a middle school social studies teacher in Green Bay, about an hour from his parent's home. Meanwhile, Elaine became a valuable substitute teacher in the Green Bay district.

Early last September, while perusing a copy of TODAY'S EDUCATOR in the teacher's lounge Michael spied an article entitled: "Sabbaticals: Not Just for College Profs." The Jefferson Foundation was offering $10,000 sabbatical grants to high school, junior high, and middle school teachers who had completed at least twenty years of teaching. One hundred of these grants would be available to teachers throughout the nation. He noted that grant proposals were to be submitted to the Foundation by December 1st with the winners to be announced the following March. And that the sabbaticals were to be completed no more than six months after this announcement.

When Michael and Elaine sat down for supper that evening, he told her about the opportunity. "Go for it," she said. "The district wants me to teach remedial reading next summer, anyhow." So with Elaine's blessing Michael completed the extensive application process.

Evidently the foundation liked his proposed project – "What's Happening to the Family Dairy Farm?" -- for on March 15th he received word from the Jefferson Foundation that he was among those to receive a sabbatical grant for the upcoming summer. Michael's plan was quite simple: He would spend two weeks touring the dairy farming areas of the state. Intending to proceed along the back roads he would stop to visit "the locals" and ask them how their lives were being affected by all the changes that had been occurring during the past several years. He would stop at feed mills and grain elevators, village restaurants and implement dealerships where he knew farmers were apt to gather. And of course, he would stop at some farms as well. From the information he was gleaning, Michael was hoping to define the common challenges faced by those he visited, and to discover the ways those farmers were confronting those challenges.

The Jefferson Foundation required only two reports from its grantees: a brief summary of how the grant money was spent, and a two to three-page essay indicating how the grantee was impacted by the sabbatical experience. The Foundation was very clear in indicating that the primary goals of their sabbatical program were rest, renewal and personal enrichment for the grantees; and that any formal research was optional.

Yet Michael was eager to do a little research. He hadn't done any since his Masters' thesis at Kent State, and he now relished the opportunity to do some research that took him – not in the stacks of a library – but out "into the field." Also, his principal and superintendent were pleased that he was engaging in an experience that thy felt might be re-energizing for him. They were well aware of the burnout that was becoming all too common among many long term teachers. So too, depending on what Michael discovered, they wondered if his efforts might bring some acclaim to Gardner School and the Green Bay district.

Now Michael reached the end of the long driveway leading to the house that bore such a resemblance to his childhood home. He stopped his red Ford pickup, got out, and as he walked toward the front door, a collie suddenly appeared, barking loudly and sniffing at his heals. When he reached the set of six steps leading to the front door, the door opened, and a woman appeared. Standing in the doorway, she looked to be in her 60's.

"Laddie, behave!" she yelled.

"Hello." said Michael as he stood at the base of the steps: "My name is Michael Lattimore."

"Yes?" the woman responded.

"I was driving along the road and noticed your house. I was struck by its similarity to my childhood home in Manitowoc County. Your house resembles it so much I just had to stop."

"Is that so?" said the woman in baggy brown slacks, a rather loose-fitting sweatshirt, and a green and gold plaid apron.

Beginning to warm up a bit to the stranger, she continued: "So you grew up on the farm?"

"No. Not exactly. I grew up out in the country. We had a half dozen acres; had some chickens and ducks, a nice little orchard, but no cattle. We were surrounded by dairy farms."

The woman -- taking a careful assessment of the stranger dressed in blue jeans, a sweatshirt bearing the name Lakeland College, and Nike running shoes and wearing a wedding band on his left hand -- began feeling much more at ease with this stranger standing at the base of her front steps.

Never ashamed of her religious convictions

and practices, she said rather bluntly: "Funny thing... Last night I was reading my devotions – something I try to do every night before bed – and it said something about 'welcoming strangers.'" With a restrained chuckle, she went on: "I guess that means I shouldn't run you off the property. I'm Linda Erickson. Come on in and take a load off your feet. Joe, my husband, called a couple of minutes ago on his cell, said he's done chopping, and he'll be here in a minute or two. He can tell you all about the house."

Stepping inside the front door, Michael took a quick look around. "This is amazing. I feel like I'm almost back in my childhood home. Your staircase and your little room over there – your den I assume – are just like those in the house I was raised."

Linda replied, "This farm has been in Joe's family for five generations. It was his great-great grandpa who built it; that is, if you're interested in hearing about it.

"O, I hear Joe coming in the back door now."

"Whose pickup is parked in the front yard?" came Joe's booming voice from another room. "Come in the front room, Joe, we've got company."

As Joe appeared, Linda announced: "Joe, this is Michael. He was driving down the road and noticed our place. He said it reminds him of his childhood home near Manitowoc."

Joe listened somewhat cautiously as Linda continued: "I told him the farm has been in the family for five generations and that you could give him the history of the place."

Joe briefly looked Michael up and down and then extended his hand to the visitor and said: "I'm Joe Erickson. Glad to meet you, Michael."

"The pleasure is mine."

"So what's it you want to know about this old house and the family farm?"

"Whatever you want to share. But I need to tell you...... I'm not only interested in your house and farm, but I've been given a sabbatical grant to study the changes that have gone on in rural life over the past twenty-five to thirty years, and how those changes have been affecting rural folks like yourselves. You see, I grew up over by the lakeshore, moved away after graduating from college, and then didn't move back until a few years ago. And when I did, I could not help but notice all the changes."

"You say you are doing a sabbatical. Isn't that what college professors get so they can do some research?

"I believe that's often the case?" responded Michael.

"So you teach?"

"Yes, but not at the college level. I taught history to high school students in Ohio for twenty years, and now I'm a middle school social studies teacher in Green Bay."

Leaning back in his recliner, Joe began: "Let me tell you first about the farm. This farm has been in the Erickson family since the late 1860's. That's when my great great grandpa Olaf came from – as they say around here --- the old country, Norway, and settled here. At first, he grew a wheat crop. But wheat rust disease and the infestation of chinch bugs changed everything. By the time he passed it down to his son, also named Olaf, it was a dairy farm. And we Ericksons have been doing it ever since; my great grandpa Olaf, my grandpa, my Mom and Dad and now Linda and me.

"Grandpa expanded it from the original 80 acres to 160 when he bought out the neighboring farm. And Dad purchased an additional hundred acres just down the road when he came back from world War II. Along with the additional acreage he increased the herd size. When we bought the farm from Dad in the early eighties, we were milking about fifty-five head. It was a rough time for so many farmers around here – as I am sure you must remember. Interest rates on borrowing were sky high. Many farmers had to sell out. They lost not only their farms and their livelihood, but their way of life. All I can say is good thing we worked something out with Dad regarding our payments so that we could afford it."

Michael listened intently as Joe went on: "We're now milking eighty-five cows and we farm about 450 acres. We own about 300 and rent the rest. We got ourselves a hired hand about ten years ago when it was getting to be too much for Linda and me. And it's worked out OK. That really saved us about five years ago when my knees went out. Had to have both of them done.

"Michael, this farm is not just a farm; not a 'business' as some would call it. Like I said a moment ago: It's a way of life – our way life; I might even go on to say, it has been our life. But you, being raised in dairy country over by Lake Michigan, I'm sure you know what I mean?"

"I sure do, Joe."

"And this house... it's old. But it's home. It's the only home I've ever known. There have been improvements over the years – things like indoor plumbing, wiring, new windows and doors. Carpeting in some of the rooms. And we're probably on our fifth or sixth roof by now. But these wooden floors, original, the studding – all original, and the plaster walls – original. The wood trim boards? All original."

"Looking at your place from the outside -- with all the gables, and the placement of the windows and doors -- it's remarkable how similar it is to the house I lived in during my childhood and youth."

"Why don't you join us for supper, Michael?" Linda interjected. "We can keep visiting. We don't get too much company these days and it's nice having you."

"I don't want to intrude," Michael responded. But then, sensing what appeared to be a look of disappointment on Linda's face, he continued: "That would be just fine, as long as I'm not being too much of a bother."

"No bother at all. We often have our big meal – our dinner – mid-day. That is, on the days I am not working in the morning. I suppose that mid-day big dinner is still a carryover from earlier days. Before you came, I was just fixing some summer sausage sandwiches and we've got some left-over coleslaw and potato salad. It's not much, but again, we usually go bigger at lunch time."

Michael was glad for the invitation. Yes, he had wanted to know the history of the farm, but he also wanted to talk about how all the changes in agriculture were affecting them. And he had yet to steer the conversation in that direction.

Moments later the three of them gathered around the small kitchen table. For some reason Michael had expected a larger table – the kind in the days when a threshing crew of eight or ten folks would plop down after several hours of strenuous labor.

On the table was spread the announced menu of sandwiches, coleslaw and potato salad. When Linda sat down and appeared to bow her head, she asked Michael if he would be offended if she offered grace.

"Of course not," said Michael.

So Linda continued: "From your bounty we have been blessed, O Lord. Thank you, for what we are about to eat. May it strengthen us to serve you and others. Amen."

With the blessing said, Joe announced: "Dig in!"

After a few bites, Michael remarked: "Wow! This is the best potato salad I've ever eaten."

"Thank you. It' a recipe handed down from my grandmother. She was a terrific cook and baker. You should have had her lefsa."

Finally, getting to the reason why he was making his trip in the first place, Michael asked: "I know how this farm has been in the family for what, over 150 years, and you, Joe, have been in this house since your birth, but I'm also interested in how have you have coped with all changes that have been happening in these last twenty-five to thirty years?"

"Twenty-five to thirty years? Heck; things have been changing since before I was born. Maybe the changes just seem accelerated in the past two or three decades. I remember as a kid, we'd still haul our milk down to the factory – the cheese factory – in those large, heavy cans that we loaded in the back of an old flatbed truck. You know the cans I'm talking about: Folks often use as front porch decorations or put a pole in them and attach their mailboxes. Might even call it some kind of fad. Back then there was a cheese factory every few miles, and I might add, a tavern, too. But those days are gone."

Suddenly Joe's demeanor changed, and he continued: "I'll tell you what really fries my bacon: Milk prices. And I'm not talking about what you have to pay for a gallon of milk when you go to the store; I'm talking about what we – the producers -- get paid per hundred. For a hundred pounds of it. You're never quite sure what you're going to get. What we get certainly hasn't kept pace with our expenses – gas, equipment, repairs, and a list of God knows what else tends to break down every year. There used to be a 'rule of thumb' that milk prices would reflect the cost of a postage stamp. When postage stamps were one cent, milk price was a dollar per hundred; when the postage stamp was three cents, the price of milk was about three dollars per hundred. Well now a postage stamp is fifty-five cents, but the price we get for our milk is far from fifty-five bucks per hundred. It has fluctuated from around seventeen to twenty dollars for the past fifteen, twenty years."

"I keep hearing that from everyone I've been

talking to," Michael responded.

"Joe, in my travels these past few days I keep seeing these huge dairy operations – those that milk one or two thousand head or more. How have these farms affected you and other smaller family farms?"

"I can think of two things right away: We smaller guys have a hard time competing with them for labor. Thankfully Sam, our hired hand, has continued to be very loyal to us. And, as I mentioned, we rent some cropland. These huge operations have to rent a lot of land; and we often find ourselves competing with them for these rental lands; we don't need to rent as much, so we've got to pay more per acre. That hits us pretty hard, too.

"We thought about going big time a few years back. Get more cows, rent more land, buy bigger equipment, put up some free stall barns. Hire at least one more hand. But the more we thought about it, we realized we didn't want to assume that much debt. Then my knees went out and we were sure we made the right decision. My gosh, I'm kind of an old-fashioned guy. I still give each of my girls a name and call her by it. Can you imagine trying to remember the names of a thousand milk cows? I guess I don't want them to be simply a number on an ear tag or computer chip."

Michael, listening intently, finally spoke: "Sounds to me like you made the right decision."

Joe had more to say: "Yes, dairy farming has

more than its fair share of challenges. Probably always has. Then there's the weather. It's a crap shoot and that's why I always say that farmers have been gamblers long before those casinos started popping up all over the place. You plant seed in the ground, and you do so with the hope that it will germinate and grow and get enough sun and rain and produce a good crop. But when you put it in the ground, you have no idea what will happen – you can only hope and pray you'll get a good yield.

"Something else I've got to mention: You remember the 80's. The soaring interest rates for borrowing back then and the drought in '88 wiped out a lot of us farmers. Truth is – even with that break Mom and Dad were giving us with regard to the interest we were paying, I don't think we'd have made it had it not for Linda doing her work at the greenhouse in Darlington."

Linda finally jumped in: "I work there a few days a week in April, May and June and then around the holiday season. It helps us make 'ends meet.' And then I always liked math, so I do some bookkeeping for a couple of nearby farm families. Plus you may have noticed coming in, I've got a huge garden, and ever since I was a little girl and helped my Mom, I have loved gardening and canning vegetables. Saves us a bundle each year."

Joe still had more to say: "The other day I was talking with my lifelong buddy, Clarence. He runs a dairy operation a couple of miles down the road that's been in his family for about as long as this one's been in ours. He decided to expand about twenty years ago. He did all the things we thought about doing. They're doing OK. But he said something interesting. He said all the technology makes work easier, but you have to do more to keep up. He said, 'It's like a dog chasing its tail.' He said that with all the advancements, especially in nutrition, he's been able to get more milk per cow. But even that can be a slippery slope because you don't want a glut in the market. You know what happens then? We get less per hundred. It's bad enough as it is."

With his head spinning from the information Joe and Linda had shared with him – some of which he had been hearing during his visits with other farmers the past few days – Michael said: "Joe and Linda, thank you. That's exactly the kind of information I am hoping to gather – a thoughtful assessment of life on the farm." They finished supper and

Linda suggested they return to the front room where she would bring them all the last of the coffee.

"I'll join you there in a minute, Michael," said Joe, "but first I've got to get some of these left-overs out to Laddie. That dog will eat anything you put in front of him."

As Michael entered the living room, he saw a small table that he had previously overlooked. It contained a couple of 8 X 10 inch frames with photographs. One showed Joe and Linda. It looked like it had been taken a few years back. They appeared considerably more robust; but then, noticing how they seemed to pick at their food during supper he wondered if they were dieting. The other was a photo of a young family. He assumed the woman to be their daughter, for he noted several facial resemblances. Along with the woman was a good-looking young man – her husband he assumed -- and a small child.

By the time Michael sat down and Joe joined him, Linda was there with coffee for the two of them. After she returned from putting the coffee pot in the kitchen, Michel announced: "You haven't told me about your family. I could not help but notice the picture. I assume, from her facial features... your daughter, her husband and a grandchild?"

Suddenly the mood of the entire room darkened. With tears welling up in his eyes and his voice choking, Joe responded: "Black ice. Do you know about black ice?"

"Yes, growing up over by Lake Michigan, I've

experienced my fair share of it."

Michael detected soft sobs coming from Linda, and he wondered what "can of worms" he had opened.

Gaining a little composure, Joe continued: "It was that damned black ice that did it. They are gone. All three of them. Killed in a car wreck fifteen months ago. Returning from a parent-teacher conference. They were on a road they had driven hundreds of times before. The car behind them said they were only going about 40 but hit a patch of black ice, went off the road and slid down an embankment and square into a large black walnut tree near the bottom of the ravine. Only tree in the whole area and they had to hit it. Five feet one way or the other and they would have been OK. Sheriff said it was the freakiest accident he had ever witnessed in all his years with the department – as a deputy and then as sheriff."

"Wow, I am so sorry."

"It's not your fault. It was that damned black ice."

Sniffing her nose, Linda reported: "They were only in their 30's. Jane is, or I should say, was thirty-five; and Jack was thirty-seven.

They met at UW – River Falls. Jane majored in elementary ed and Jack in animal science. Thankfully Jane got a job teaching in the district next county over; and Jack worked for Ag Service in Platteville. Both had good jobs and were raising a beautiful daughter, Annie."

Trying to hold back more tears, Linda continued: "Our beautiful granddaughter, Annie. Just doesn't seem fair."

Joe went on: "Can you believe it, Michael? Somebody at the visitation on the night before the funeral came up to me and said: 'You know – everything happens for a reason. It just must have been their time.' Their time? Jane and Jack in their 30's and little Annie only five. No way! I could have slugged the guy. And then when I was in a stall in the bathroom, I heard that same guy telling someone else in the rest room: 'They – meaning us – are just going to accept this as God's will.' What the heck was he saying? What kind of God would will that two hard-working, loving parents and their beautiful innocent child be here one moment and then gone the next? I don't buy it. No. way! If that's true, I want nothing to do with such a God."

Michael, searching for the appropriate words, simply mumbled: "I agree."

Linda chimed in: "Delores, from our church, had the audacity to tell me: 'You know, Linda, God doesn't give us any more than we can bear?'

I haven't been able to bring myself to speak with Delores ever since, and it's been well over a year since the accident."

"I keep trying to convince myself that these folks really did not know what to say and were probably trying to make some sense out of something that makes absolutely no sense at all." said Joe, his voice filled with resignation.

"Maybe so. But you and I know how much those words hurt back then and still do," said Linda.

Michael began to sense why Joe and Linda had only picked at their food and had a pretty good idea as to their obvious weight loss from the time that photograph had been taken a few years earlier. Who can eat when your insides are filled with heartache and anguish? he thought.

"This grief, this deep, deep sadness. It just doesn't seem to pass." Joe offered. "I wonder if it will ever go away. I might be fine for a day or two, but then it comes rushing back. I can be out on the tractor enjoying the fresh air doing some chopping or something, and then it hits me like a giant wave, throwing me back into a deep sadness."

After a few seconds of silence, Michael offered a thought: "It's interesting you should use the word 'wave.' When my Dad passed away several years ago, I thought I was 'over it' a couple of months later. After all, I reminded myself that he had lived a good life, and after having survived a major heart attack as a forty-year-old, he lived another thirty-five years in relatively good health. Sometimes I thought I was through with the sadness, but then, like you said, it would wash over me, too, like a giant wave. Growing up close to Lake Michigan I could not help to think that my grief was like the waves on the lake. One day, my grief would seem like rather gentle waves lapping up on the shore; the next day, it was more like large waves bounding up on the shore with great force; the next, kind of gentle again, only to be followed by another day of large, strong waves. Eventually, however, the episodes of the larger, overpowering waves of grief began to lessen and come less frequently. Yes Joe, grief seems to come in waves."

"I only wish there wouldn't be so damned many of them."

"It must have been awful. I can understand how you must have been devastated.," Michael continued.

"Have been devastated? I still am! Awful? It still is. My farm work? Sometimes I think I'm just going through the motions. But it keeps my mind occupied. And other than Linda, I often feel it's all I've got left. Then on top of all this there's something else. Maybe this is a little selfish. But I always hoped we could pass the farm down to Jane and Jack. Jack always said he didn't want to get tied down with milking, but he did mention once that he wouldn't mind raising calves and heifers. But now, that dream is dashed, too."

Then Linda added: "All those stages of grief folks talk about. I don't know if I've moved through any of them. I still think some afternoon Jane is going to come through the door to announce something that little Annie did or something that happened in her classroom. Somebody said I'm still 'in denial.' But I guess our minds play tricks on us like that."

A moment passed and Michael gently offered: "Linda and Joe, if you want, tell me a little more about Jane and Jack and little Annie."

"You really want to know?" Linda asked. "We shouldn't be burdening you with our troubles."

"Yes, I'd be eager to hear; I bet you have some special memories."

"Oh I sure I do, but I wouldn't know where to begin," said Linda.

"Anywhere you want to."

"Well then, let me start with little Annie. She is, oh, I should say was such a smart little tyke.

One day, she had just turned two, she came bouncing in the door – she never walked, she always ran -- and said, 'Grammy, Grammy,' and went on to sing that alphabet song. She was so proud of herself. And I was proud of her, too. Numbers? By the time she was two and a half, she could rattle them off as well. One through twenty, but always seemed to get stuck at thirteen."

"I need to tell you a story about Annie, too." Joe blurted out: "I suppose she was barely two, I came in from the barn and Linda had the radio on. They were playing a good old oldie -- some song with a pretty good beat. What does Annie do? She comes up to me and looks up and into my eyes and says: 'Grampa, dance with me.' Talk about my old Scandinavian heart melting."

"Jane," Linda said, "you could not have asked for a better daughter. She wasn't perfect; but she was always a good kid. She liked school; took it seriously. When she went out with friends in high school, she would always check in with us to tell us she got home. But one time we had to ground her for two weeks: She said she'd call us when the dance was over, and she started for home. But she didn't. We worried sick. She finally made it home about midnight and said rather casually: 'Oh, I just forgot to call.' But 'rules are rules' we told her, and so we grounded her for two weeks. Nearly broke our hearts."

"Want to know one of my favorite memories?" asked Joe.

"Sure," replied Michael.

"It happened on the night of Jane's birth. It was a full moon. After she was born and Linda came back to her room, the nurses did all the things with Jane they have to do after a baby is born – and then they brought Jane into Linda's room. She was a chunky little bundle -- all wrapped up in a soft pink blanket. Then the nurse told me if I wanted to hold her, I had to put on a gown and wear some gloves. I put the stuff on, reached out for her, took her in my arms and for some reason, I walked over to the window. A full moon was shining. And I told her, 'Jane, look at the moon shining down on you.' She was only a couple of hours old – if that.

"Twenty-four years later it was my honor to escort her down the aisle when she married Jack."

"Speaking of Jack, what kind of son-in-law was he?" asked Michael.

"Jack? Let me tell you about Jack" said Joe as he leaned back in his recliner. "I wasn't sure what to think when Jane called and said she was bringing a boy home with her for the weekend and told us to be on our best behavior. 'A college boy – probably somebody from the Twin Cities or some other big city who didn't know the difference between a pitchfork and a garden spade,' I thought. Anyhow, I always assumed she and that Hagen boy she dated in high school would eventually get together. He was a nice boy. We know his parents well. A good family; and he always seemed to treat Jane very well. But I guess that was not to be. Well, Jack comes home with Jane late one Friday afternoon and the first thing he does is to go into the guest room to change his clothes. He even comes out wearing a pair of barn boots. 'And just what do you think you're doing?' Jane asked him in a rather authoritarian voice. 'I'm going out to help your Dad with the milking,' he said matter-of-factly. Needless to say, Linda and I were impressed, but weren't sure if he was just trying to score some early points. Well, if that was his motive, it worked.

"Speaking of milking. I mentioned I had to have my knees done a few years ago. During this whole process – surgery, recovery and rehab time – Jack drove over each morning before work and each evening to help Sam with the milking.

"Oh, and one more story: I always wanted to go fishing way Up North. Around Hayward or Eagle River or somewhere where they catch those big muskies. One Father's Day Jack gets it all worked out so that just the two of us – Jack and me – could spend a couple of days on a lake just outside Boulder Junction – the place that calls itself 'the Musky Capital of the World.' We didn't catch any muskies. Never even had one follow up the bait. But we did land a couple of nice northerns. Boy did we ever have fun. Just us boys."

"I got one better than that," announced Linda. "One day, and this is before Annie was born, Jane was getting all worried about how she looked. She had gained something like forty pounds during her pregnancy and never wanted to have her picture taken. So Jack calls me up one night and asks: 'Why don't you and Jane go over to Dubuque and have one of those facials?' I was surprised he knew what the word meant. He said that the two of us should take off some Saturday, and he would come out and do what needed to be done around here. And that's exactly what happened. He came over about 8 A.M. one Saturday morning, took over doing the breakfast dishes, made sure he and Joe had something for lunch, and when Jane and I got back home at 5 P.M. we had the big meal of the day. He had roasted a turkey, made mashed potatoes, dressing, and green beans. He did, however, bring a store-bought pie. I continued to tease him about that last item. And it wasn't even Thanksgiving. I remember Jane's words to him after dinner: 'Jack, I might be eight months pregnant; but today, you made me feel like a queen.' He was a man who treated us and our daughter and later, little Annie so well. Oh, I do miss him – all of them – so much."

Michael, in a kind, deliberate voice responded: "Thank you both for sharing your stories. They were beautiful. You have such wonderful remembrances. It seems you have much to be thankful for."

"I suppose we do," a subdued Joe responded.

"Enough about us, Michael. Here we've been telling you all our troubles, and never once did we ask you about your family. I see from the ring on your hand, you're married?"

"Yes, Elaine and I just celebrated our twenty-eighth anniversary. She's a substitute teacher in and around Green Bay. And this summer she's teaching remedial reading."

"And children?" asked Linda.

"Two. Both grown. Our daughter Sarah has always had a big heart and so she works in inner city Milwaukee at a non for profit that seeks to provide decent housing for those in need. Our son, Simon, followed in his mother's footsteps. He's an elementary school teacher. He teaches third and fourth grades in Ripon."

"Michael, are they married, and do you and Elaine have any grandchildren?" asked Joe.

"Yes – they're married. But no. No grandchildren yet. But we're hoping pretty soon."

"Well, folks I really need to be going. You have been great hosts. Thank you for your wonderful hospitality. It has been a real pleasure spending this time with you."

"The pleasure has been all ours, hasn't it, Linda?"

"It sure has. Michael, if you ever get this way again, do stop in."

"And if you ever get up our way, please look us up. I'll take you past my old childhood home. You can see for yourself how much it resembles your place."

"Goodbye then," said Michael as he stood and grasped Joe's hand for a firm handshake.

"Thank you, Linda" he said as she reached out to embrace him.

"Adios, amigo! Travel safely." Joe said lightheartedly as he opened the door and let Michael pass through.

And with that, Michael walked down the porch steps, softly patted Laddie on the head, got into his pickup and drove out the long driveway and back out onto the County Highway N, intending to drive to Platteville where he would spend the night.

Linda returned to the kitchen to tidy up a bit and do a few dishes while Joe went to the barn to check on Sam who had just finished the evening's milking.

Within an hour, Joe and Linda returned to the living room – Joe taking his place in his recliner and Linda getting comfortable in the rocker by a large floor lamp. Linda picked up a nearby book of crossword puzzles and began working on one. Joe, meanwhile, skimmed the sports section of the WISCONSIN STATE JOURNAL that had come in the mail earlier in the day. When he finished that, it was time to thumb through the MIDWEST DAIRYMAN. Both Joe and Linda were unusually quiet, almost like they were in deep thought.

Then Linda reached into her nearby knitting basket and finished a few rows on an afghan she had started a couple of weeks earlier. She soon put it down and read her nightly devotional material.

Linda finally broke the silence: "Hey Joe, Michael sure seemed like a nice man."

Joe replied: "He sure did."

"Well, I'm ready for bed," Linda announced.

"I'll be there in a few minutes," said Joe.

It had been a long day. Joe had been up since 5 A.M. and Linda had put in a few hours at the greenhouse in the forenoon.

Despite being tired, neither could not get to sleep. After about an hour, Joe told Linda, "I think I need to go check on the girls." Linda wasn't surprised, for she long lost count of how many times Joe would rather abruptly leave the house to check on the cows. He said something about not being sure if he had secured the pasture gate and he didn't want to spend half of the next morning tracking cows who seem to find every opening. Linda finally drifted off to sleep about an hour later.

But Joe did not check on his girls. Rather, he went to his recliner, and, looking out the window into the moonlit yard and pasture, lost himself in thought. Finally after about two hours he returned to bed and fell asleep easily.

The alarm was set to go off at 5 A.M. as it had for every day for the past forty years. Linda and Joe both awakened a few moments before the alarm sounded.

"Linda," asked Joe, "are you awake?"

"I am now, Joe. No. I'm just kidding. I've been awake a few minutes."

"Linda, I got a rather strange sensation yesterday afternoon when we were talking with Michael. It wasn't anything bad, just a little something I can't explain. It's when we were talking about the kids and Michael said: 'It sounds like you have a lot to be thankful for.' I just felt something – for a brief instant -- but then didn't think too much about it until I came to bed. I figure that's why I couldn't get to sleep last night. I said I was going out to check on the girls, but instead I just went down to the recliner – I guess to just sit in the quiet to think. I didn't turn on the TV, but instead, I turned my chair so I could look out the window into the moonlight. And for the first time since the accident, my alone time was not flooded with intense sadness. I thought about Jane and the way she used to swing on that old tire I attached on the oak tree; and instead of crying, I found myself smiling. I thought about how nervous she was when she and the Hagen boy went to their prom. She was beautiful. I used to cry when I had such thoughts. Last night, I just smiled. I remembered when I suggested to her that I give her driving lessons, and how she said to me: 'Dad, do you really think I need driving lessons? You've been letting me drive the tractor since I was twelve.' And I found myself still smiling. Linda, the memories were good. I found myself smiling in the darkness and I really felt thankful for all those good times."

Looking deeply into Joe's eyes, Linda replied: "Funny you should say all this. When you got up, I didn't get to sleep either. At least, not for another hour or so. I was also thinking about what Michael said; and it got me thinking about how much we have to be thankful for. I started remembering all the 4-H calves Jane took to the fair. Remember her first blue ribbon. She was only ten. I too, had to smile. I remembered her wedding day and how she almost got 'cold feet,' and how you assured her that she was marrying a very good man. And indeed he was. He treated her and us well. I remembered holding little Annie for the first time and I recalled those wonderful moments I spent reading to her and all the times she fell asleep on my lap. I guess I started focusing not so much on what we lost and no longer have but thought about how thankful I am for what we did have. Yes, I still want the three of them back. And I would do anything to have them back."

Reaching out to clasp Joe's hand, she announced: "But Joe, we did have them. If only for a while. But that time we had was very, very good. And yes, I am thankful for it. And it took this absolute stranger to start me thinking this way. Do you think, Joe, that maybe we're beginning to turn a corner on our grief?"

"I don't know, Linda, but I hope so."

"Well, I better get out to the girls. Despite all those changes on the farm we talked about yesterday with Michael, they still don't milk themselves. And speaking of the girls, I know the day will come when we'll have to sell them, when they'll be too much for us. I got to thinking about that too, before I came back to bed. Maybe I'll be OK with that. In fact, maybe we can work something out with Sam. But not just yet."

"Oh, by the way, Joe, I thought the reason I let Michael in the house was that I knew you were on your way in. I don't think I would have done so if you were still in the field. Anyway, my instincts told me I could trust him.

"But Joe, there's something else: Night before last in my devotions I read something about welcoming strangers. And then it said something very interesting: "When we welcome strangers, we may be entertaining angels without even knowing it."

"Are you saying that Michael is an angel?" Linda.

"Well, his name IS Michael, isn't it?"

Lawrence Balleine

5711 Koller Circle
Monticello, Wisconsin 53570
balleine@tds.net
608-938-4367

Lawrence Balleine is a retired Congregational/United Church of Christ pastor who resides in south central Wisconsin. He and his wife, Pansy, are the proud parents of two adult children – Erin and Travis – and four grandchildren. In addition to spending time with his grandchildren, Lawrence continues to do "pulpit supply," and enjoys multiple outdoor activities. He is an honor graduate of Lakeland University and the Divinity School of Vanderbilt University. Throughout his career, he has had a passion for rural/small town ministry.

www.ingramcontent.com/pod-product-compliance
Lightning Source LLC
Chambersburg PA
CBHW070453170726
48291CB00005B/1740

* 9 7 8 1 9 4 9 8 8 8 8 5 0 *